ACTION LAB ENTERTAINMENT PROUDLY PRESENTS

Vamplets

WRITTEN BY

GAYLE MIDDLETON
&
DAVE DWONCH

ART BY

AMANDA CORONADO
WITH
BILL BLANKENSHIP

EDITED BY: DARYL BANNER AND BETH DOBIN-COLLAKU

BRYAN SEATON - PUBLISHER
KEVIN FREEMAN - PRESIDENT
SHAWN PRYOR - VP DIGITAL MEDIA
SHAWN GABBORIN - EDITOR IN CHIEF
DAVE DWONCH - CREATIVE DIRECTOR
JASON MARTIN - EDITOR
CHAD CICCONI - BASS PLAYER IN THE MUSICAL MAYHEM SOCIETY
COLLEEN BOYD - ASSOCIATE EDITOR
JAMAL IGLE & KELLY DALE - DIRECTORS OF MARKETING

CHAPTER 3

"PANDEMONIUS DIRGE"

WRITTEN BY GAYLE MIDDLETON AND DAVE DWONCH
DRAWN BY AMANDA CORONADO
COLOR ART BY BILL BLANKENSHIP
LETTERED BY DAVE DWONCH

*WHERE ARE THEY HEADED? FIND OUT IN VAMPLETS: THE LEGEND OF THE GHOST PONY #1!

THE NEXT MORNING.

GAHHH!! HOW LONG HAVE YOU BEEN HERE?!

LONGER THAN I'D PREFER, MORTAL.

I'M AFRAID I MUST REPORT THAT MR. G IS, TO SAY THE LEAST, DISAPPOINTED IN YOU.

UH, IS THIS A DRAWING? IT LOOKS CUTE!

AND IN GLOOMVANIA, CUTE IS BAD, DESTINY!

DON'T YOU KNOW THE RULES??

THREE STRIKES AND YOU'RE OUT!

SIGH.

YOU MUST MAKE AMENDS, DESTINY HARPER.

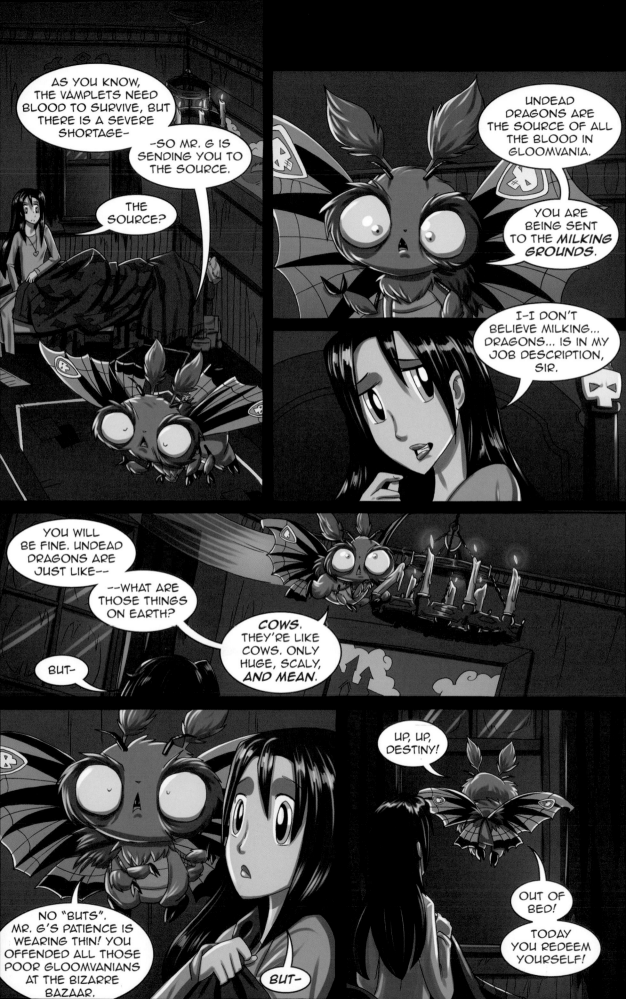

CHAPTER

4

"HOW TO MILK YOUR DRAGON"

WRITTEN BY GAYLE MIDDLETON AND DAVE DWONCH
DRAWN BY AMANDA CORONADO
COLOR ART BY BILL BLANKENSHIP
LETTERED BY DAVE DWONCH

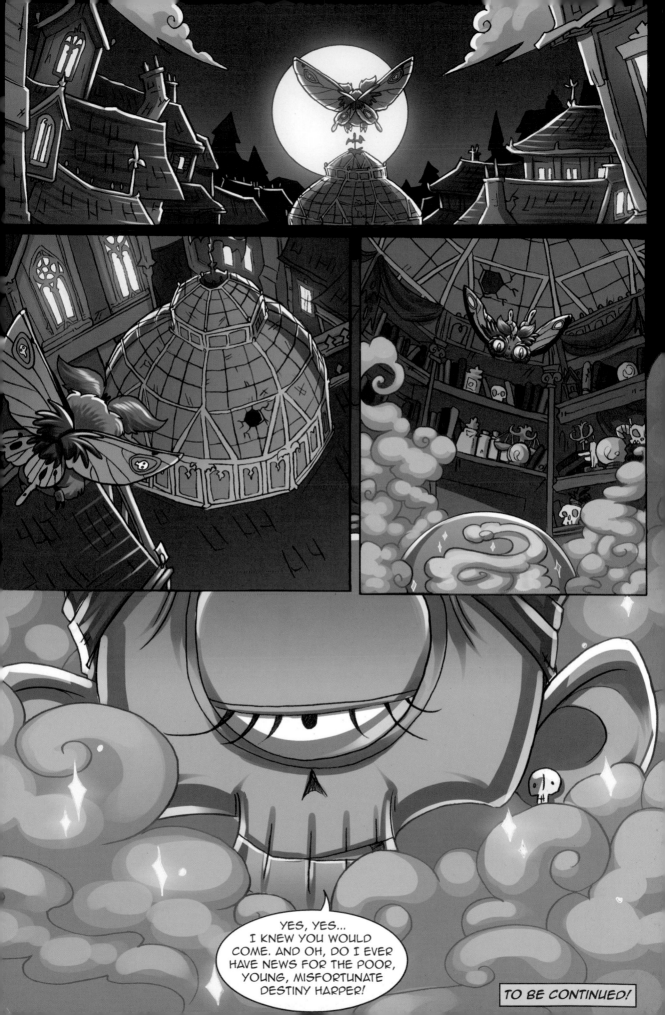

YES, YES...
I KNEW YOU WOULD
COME. AND OH, DO I EVER
HAVE NEWS FOR THE POOR,
YOUNG, MISFORTUNATE
DESTINY HARPER!

TO BE CONTINUED!

STANDARD
COVER BY

AMANDA
CORONADO
&
WILLIAM
BLANKENSHIP

VARIANT
COVER BY

GAYLE
MIDDLETON
&
WILLIAM
BLANKENSHIP